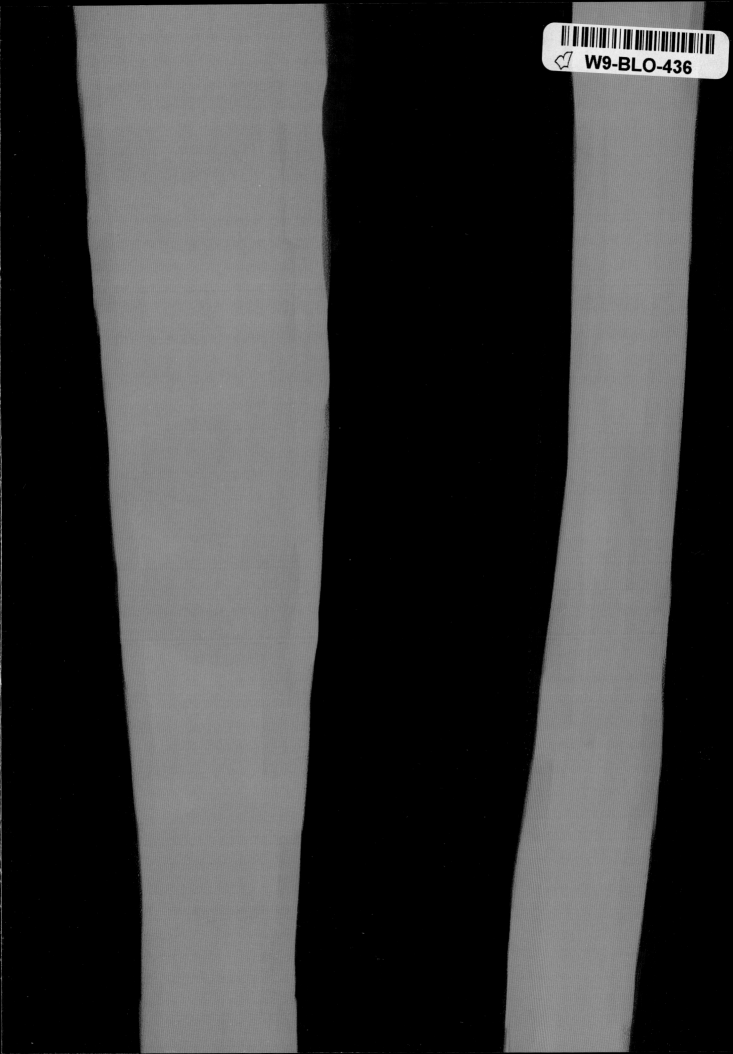

W9-BLO-436

for
Anya,
just the
way
you are

SIMON & SCHUSTER BOOKS FOR YOUNG READERS
An imprint of Simon & Schuster Children's Publishing Division
1230 Avenue of the Americas, New York, New York 10020
Copyright © 2016 by Mike Boldt
SIMON & SCHUSTER BOOKS FOR YOUNG READERS is a trademark of Simon & Schuster, Inc.
For information about special discounts for bulk purchases, please contact Simon & Schuster Special Sales at
1-866-506-1949 or business@simonandschuster.com.
The Simon & Schuster Speakers Bureau can bring authors to your live event. For more information or to book an event,
contact the Simon & Schuster Speakers Bureau at 1-866-248-3049 or visit our website at www.simonspeakers.com.
Book design by Mike Boldt
The text for this book is set in Bitstream Cooper.
The illustrations for this book are digitally rendered.
Manufactured in China
0416 SCP
First Edition
2 4 6 8 10 9 7 5 3 1
Library of Congress Cataloging-in-Publication Data
Boldt, Mike, author, illustrator.
A tiger tail / Mike Boldt.—1st edition.
pages cm
Anya awakens to discover she has grown a tiger tail, and it just happens to be her very first day of school.
ISBN 978-1-4814-4885-7 (hardcover : alk. paper)
ISBN 978-1-4814-4886-4 (eBook)
[1. First day of school—Fiction.] I. Title.
PZ7.B635863Tig 2016
[E]—dc23
2015029701

Anya woke one day . . .

only to discover

that overnight, she had grown . . .

A Tiger Tail!

by Mike Boldt

Simon & Schuster Books for Young Readers
New York   London   Toronto   Sydney   New Delhi

THE BEST Hair styles
4 Girlz !!

Yes, a tiger tail.
Not like a ponytail
or pigtails.
A TIGER tail.

Le Tiger

Tail

La Girl

No tail !

A tiger tail was a DISASTER.
She absolutely could NOT be seen.

Unfortunately, that wasn't an option as it was Anya's first day of school.

Are girls with tiger tails even allowed to go to school? What would the other kids say?

Her mom said, "It goes so nicely with your hair. It brings out your fun, wild side!"

That may be, Anya thought, *but this was a problem on her* back *side*.

Her dad said, "I remember feeling the same way when I got glasses. Don't fret. You're exactly the same wonderful Anya you've always been."

He obviously needed new glasses.

She would have to take care of this herself.

She *tugged.*

She *pulled.*

She *squished.*

She stopped.

The tail was firmly attached.

Maybe she could hide it. Anya tried on all the
clothes in her closet . . .

at the same time.

(It would have worked,
if she didn't have to tinkle.)

Anya started to panic.

"Calm down," said her mom.
"You'll make yourself sick."

That was a good idea.

"You are so funny, Anya. The kids are going to love your sense of humor. Now hurry or you'll miss the bus."

That was another good idea.

"What a special treat!" said her dad. "Now I get to drive
you to school on your first day."

Anya realized there was only one choice for a girl with a
tiger tail. She would have to run away and join the circus.
Would it be so bad? Popcorn for dinner. Swinging on the
trapeze. Feeding peanuts to the elephants. . . .

TOO LATE.

Anya was DOOMED.

"Hi. My name is Ben."   "I'm Anya."

"Come on, Anya! We don't
want to be late on the first day."

Maybe a tiger tail wasn't so bad.

SUNNYSIDE ELEMENTARY
GRADE 1C

1/125 F5.6 ISO 400

After all, it did go well with her hair.